Metaphorosis

August 2023

Beautifully made speculative fiction

Also from Metaphorosis

<u>Metaphorosis Magazine</u>
Metaphorosis: Best of 20xx
Metaphorosis 20xx: The Complete Stories
annual issues, from 2016
Monthly issues

<u>Plant Based Press</u>
Best Vegan Science Fiction & Fantasy
annual issues, 2016-2020

from B. Morris Allen:
Chambers of the Heart: speculative stories
Susurrus
Allenthology: Volume I
Tocsin: and other stories
Start with Stones: collected stories
Metaphorosis: a collection of stories

<u>Verdage</u>
Reading 5X5 x3: Changes
Reading 5X5 x2: Duets
Score: an SFF symphony
Reading 5X5: Readers' Edition
Reading 5X5: Writers' Edition

<u>Vestige</u>
The Nocturnals, by Mariah Montoya

<u>Joyful Heave</u>
Museum Piece: an unusual collection

Metaphorosis

August 2023

edited by
B. Morris Allen

ISSN: 2573-136X (online)
ISBN: 978-1-64076-263-3 (e-book)
ISBN: 978-1-64076-264-0 (paperback)

from
Metaphorosis Publishing

Neskowin

August 2023

A Wielder Does Not Know Regret

Katherine Karch

You are walking down a winter road that carves a gentle arc through a forest of hemlock and fir. Somewhere, a brook flows along icy banks, the soft murmur of its waters slipping between wide trunks and snow-bent branches. In your hand, a folded square of paper with the following:

A request for the services of a Wielder. Take the western road from the Citadel. Do not look ahead. Do not look behind. Do not lose yourself.

Quantum variations of the message's meaning swirl upon the paper, marking its authenticity. You fold it closed, hold it tightly in your hand.

From somewhere close to the road a songbird chirps a high, two-toned note. *Phee-bee.*

The sound elicits a smile. You stop walking, head tilted toward the tiny creature, and wield. The world bends around awareness, time slowing until it is like cool honey dripping from the comb of consciousness.

Pheeeeeeeeeeee—

beeeeeeeeeee.

Eternity spirals outward, and in the endlessness of *now*, every possible variation of the bird's greeting is a joy. Delighted, you release the moment. Time flows freely once again.

A curtain of clouds is sliding into view over the treetops to the west. Their grey tones hint at snow. Barely visible behind them, the sun hangs upon a notably low zenith, and even as you hold your mind in stillness of now, nature's rhythms ebb and flow in the biology of your body. A gentle hunger tugs for attention.

It is midday.

Beside the road, a fallen pine lies blanketed in a powdery layer of snow that brushes cleanly from the rough corrugations of its bark. This is a good spot to sit and eat.

The pack you set between your feet is filled with items that invite speculation. With hunger as an anchor, though, it is safe to explore its contents. A blanket roll; wool shirt, pants, and socks. A hunting knife with a keen edge and a worn grip. A small measuring device of tarnished brass with the letters *L*, *R*, and *P* etched into one corner of the dull metal. You pull it from the pack, turn it over in your hands, set it aside.

In a folded square of linen you find several morel mushrooms. Their rich flavor sharpens the hunger in your belly, but a second folded square of linen yields a sizable cash of salted groundnuts.

There is a palm-sized book in the pack as well. Its leather cover is inscribed with the title, *Poems*. You glide your thumb along the soft and fuzzy edges of the book's pages. Words shape and stack themselves upon the paper, but you do not read them. Instead, you tuck the book back into the folds of the pack. It feels right to not spoil their undifferentiated state of totipotence.

The measuring device is cold now from lying on the ground. You use it to check the height of the sun's journey. Today, it says, is winter's solstice. The turning of the year.

With a fistful of snow, you chill the blade of the knife, draw it across your forearm alongside five matching scars. The pain anchors you, tethers you to the present, makes it possible to look beyond its boundaries, to see–if only briefly–how long it has been since you chose to become a Wielder.

Six years. There is a pinching in your chest that feels like sadness. Then, it is gone.

A strip of linen deftly tied is enough to pull the edges of the wound together and stop its bleeding. You roll down your sleeve, wipe blood from your blade, and set off again.

Evening is settling into the low places of the forest now, and a heaviness is building in your legs, a fatigue that implies a long day of walking.

Your left forearm aches.

Ahead, where the road curves and vanishes from sight, a figure stands silhouetted in the gloaming. The distance is too far to make out many details beyond the figure's stance, the wide and staggered placement of feet, the hunched uneven slant of shoulders.

"Hello," a man's voice calls out. "Are you coming from the Citadel?"

You shake your head. "I cannot look backward to answer that question."

The man tips his head like a squirrel at the sound of a snapping twig.

You are close enough now to see him clearly. He is dressed in layers of leather and fur to fend off the cold. His face is mostly hidden by a thick beard, but there is an urgency in the pull of his brows, the shape of his lips, the dark shadows beneath his eyes. He squints. Recognition haunts his features. His shoulders tense.

"It's you," he says.

A simple enough truth. "It's me."

"You are a Wielder, then."

"I am."

"I sent word to the Guild that I needed a Wielder, but..." his voice tapers into a stillness forming between you.

"Then it is good I am here." You hold up the paper in your hand, the words swirling in ever shifting fractals of meaning that only a Wielder can parse.

He tugs the back of his neck with a mittened hand, brow pinched as if in pain. "I didn't expect them to send you."

"Our Guild serves all who have need for our craft."

The light has all but left the world now. A quiet chill settles in as you regard one another—him wary and uncertain, you patient and eternal. Snowflakes begin to drift down through the evening air.

"Are you truly a Wielder?"

You smile at the wonder in his voice. "I am."

His mouth tightens as if to bite back something pressing for release. When he finally speaks, his words are stumbling. "You– I– My daughter. She's sick."

There is more, you are certain, but you accept what he tells you. "I am sorry to hear it."

"I've tried everything, but nothing's worked. I have food. A fire. A bed for the night. Will you help her?"

Such questions. You smile. "I cannot look ahead to see, but I am done walking for today."

His cabin is small but sturdily crafted, the close-set timbers deftly chinked. A season's worth of split wood is stacked beneath the roof's south-facing overhang. Smoke curls from a fieldstone chimney. The sight of it evokes a sense of comfort, of *home*. Inside, it is warm and softly lit, a single open room filled with a table, three chairs, and a wooden chest in one corner. Everything speaks of a hard but good life.

Wordless, you lean your pack by the door, then set to removing your many layers. When done, he gestures for you to sit at the small table and presents a bowl filled with something thick and steaming. It smells of carrots and onions and wild garlic scapes. Between each bite, you take in the smaller details of his home.

A copper pan and cookpot reflect the firelight like lanterns from where they hang on the wall. The wooden chest is a work of art, its edges embellished with decorative carvings that suggest a focused mind and a steady hand. Atop the chest sits a daguerreotype in an oval frame. In the image, the man stands beside a dark-haired woman in a white dress. They're both smiling, but you see whispers of doubt clinging to the edges of the woman's eyes.

"Who is she to you?" you ask.

He turns away and sets to washing the dinnerware. His voice is husky with sorrow when he answers.

"My wife."

Yes, of course.

You pull in a slow breath, noting the myriad scents filling the cabin. Sweat, wood smoke, vegetable stew simmering in the fireplace. Mink oil. Damp wool. A child's sickness, sour and sharp. There is a ladder leading to a narrow loft overhead.

The child is buried deep in a nest of old blankets. Her face glows with fever. Strands of dark hair cling to her sweat-sheened forehead. A necklace circles her throat. Six polished beads hang from its leather cord. The man comes to stand at the base of the ladder but says nothing.

"Let me see what can be done," you say.

Careful not to wake the child, you squeeze in beside her, find a comfortable position, take hold of this moment with your mind, and wield.

Reality stretches into an endless state. The child's life unfurls before you. Strings of possibility vibrate and shine in an iridescent rainbow of colors. Some tangle with your own, a tickling, pleasant sensation. No Wielder possesses the skill to touch infinity, but you can trace many of the girl's strings, heft their weight, gauge their strength and flexibility.

Time regains its linearity. The child's chest rises and falls in labored pants, and a sadness settles into your heart. You cannot resist reaching out to caress her feverish cheek.

Such a sweet young sparrow.

The thought bubbles up, unexpected, a temptation to look away from the present and lose yourself. Worse, lose the magic you possess now. Deep breath in. Slow breath out. The moment passes.

"The child's illness has taken hold deep in her lungs," you say as you climb down the ladder to the man below. "Many of her strings are collapsing."

He looks stricken, eyes shining in the firelight, brimming with tears. "There's nothing you can do, then? She's going to die?"

A silly question. Though the strings of every creature are unique, ever-shifting froths of potentiality diverging in beautiful and limitless arrays, they all share one commonality. With gentle sympathy you answer, "All threads end eventually."

"My little bird. Ever since..." He swallows hard, eyes fixed on the floor. "She's all I have left."

You should refuse. Reversing entropic decay requires perfect focus and an enormous transfer of energy. It is not without danger, even for a Master Wielder. You are only a Journeyman, but the sorrow in the man's voice is evidence of the truth in his words. It is settled, then.

"I can help you."

You settle in beside the child. Her pulse is rapid and weak beneath your fingers as you bring your thoughts to the focal point of the girl's origin. You set yourself like a fulcrum in the space between what is yet to come and what has passed, and *stretch*.

At the very center of the child, where infinite variations of a single life hum and swirl, the strings of reality are thin and fading. It is difficult work, gauging and assessing, finding threads that are both long and stable. Each transfer of energy from one potential life to another introduces uncertainty and invites a spontaneous collapse. Slowly, carefully, thread by thread, you wield. Fatigue is gnawing at your edges, so you release your attention from the girl. Time flows once again.

The angry flush of fever is withdrawing from the child's cheeks. Her pulse is settling, but her breaths sound wet as though her lungs are filled with water.

You activate your parasympathetic pathways. Rest. Recover. Wield. Thread by thread, you reshape the fabric of the child's existence. Rest. Recover. Wield. Again. Again. Again...

Daylight is easing back into the world now.

"The illness is not gone, but the girl has a wild, fierce little spirit," you tell the man. "Her possibilities are strong now."

"Thank you," he says and wraps you in a hug. There is a bed tucked beneath the cabin's loft. You accept his offer to rest, and sleep comes swiftly.

Long beams of sunlight catch in motes of dust that drift and settle across an oval portrait atop a wooden chest. A bed of glowing coals pops in the hearth. The thick aroma of molasses and peppered yams permeates the warm cabin as a man sitting by the fire lifts the lid of a cast iron pot and stirs the contents.

You stretch, rise to dress. From the loft overhead comes the sound of a small body shifting.

"Stay for dinner," the man by the hearth says.

His face gives no sign of threat, though there is a certain familiarity to his features and his voice. As a Wielder, the intuitive sense of knowing this man cannot be examined, only acknowledged.

"Thank you. I am hungry."

His smile falters, but he nods, then turns back to tend the pot above the fire. You slide into one of the three chairs at the table and watch in silence while he retrieves a pan from the wall. The pan sizzles, and the smell of grease and frying chicory root is a delight.

"What's it like?" he asks with his back to you. "The Citadel, I mean."

Your pulse quickens. There are rules that must be followed when speaking with a Wielder, and you are certain that this man knows he is breaking them.

"Why do you ask a question I cannot answer?"

"I'm sorry. It's just... it's good to see you again." He turns to set the food on the table, catching your gaze furtively.

A series of creaks and shifts from above draw your attention upward. The face of a young girl is peeking down from the loft. She is pale, thin, brown hair tangled and dirty, but her eyes are bright and curious. For several moments, long even without your magic stretching the world, the two of you regard one another. She does not speak. Instead, she regards you with an openness and a calmness befitting a member of your Guild.

"Hello, little bird," you say, then look at the man. He's gone still and is staring.

With a startling ferocity, he begins to weep. His broad shoulders sag inward. His head sinks toward his chest, and he collapses into his chair.

"You really don't remember, do you?" he cries.

"To remember is to forget. A Wielder—"

"But you weren't *always* a Wielder. You had a family. You had a *life*."

"Do I not have a life now?"

He shakes his head in frustration. "Please don't leave. You can stay here. You can stay with *us*, Lena."

That name in his voice plucks hard upon a single string, sets it vibrating with a force that bends your awareness towards it. Strings resonate, harmonize, phase with one another. A probability begins to manifest as a memory.

You stand, leave dinner untouched upon the table, retrieve your pack from beside the door. "I must go."

The man's eyes fill with anguish. "It's been six years, Lena."

He is hurting, but this hurt is a thing you cannot heal, a weight you dare not carry, a test. The strings of your reality continue to orient into parallel states, with fewer and fewer degrees of freedom. Your breath grows shallow.

"I am a Wielder. I look neither forward nor back. I am here, now, always. There is nothing to miss."

His grief overbalances, tips into anger. "That's a lie. There *is*! You had a life, a family who loved you! The Guild showed up, and—"

"Stop!"

Without conscious thought or intent, driven by the biology of your panicked body, you wield. Time slows, stops, stretches, expands, elongates, ceases.

There is only *now*.

From the loft above, the girl continues to watch, her eyes calm and without judgment. You smile up at her. She is beautiful in all her various possibilities.

Be well, little bird, you think.

Cold bites at your cheeks as you close the door on the warmth of the space within the cabin and let time flow once more.

The sun is sliding slowly downward on its journey toward the end of day. In your hand, a folded square of paper with the following:

The Citadel welcomes you, Master Wielder. Take the eastward road. Do not look ahead. Do not look behind. Do not lose yourself.

Quantum variations of the message swirl upon the paper, thus marking its authenticity. You fold it closed, hold it tightly in your hand.

As the shadows lengthen, a grey bird hops from branch to branch in a nearby tree. A smile touches your lips at the sight of a pink underbelly as it fluffs itself against the cold, black eyes curious and bright.

Phee-bee, it calls, and your whole existence catches on the sound. The center of awareness shifts, the strings of reality harmonize into the memory of a child's name and of a choice made. The world shivers, tightens, threatens to collapse into something singular.

You draw a slow, deep breath in and hold it. The moment passes, and you remain.

See Katherine Karch's story "A Wielder Does Not Know Regret" online at Metaphorosis.
If you liked it, leave a comment. Authors love that!
Remember to subscribe to our e-mail updates so you'll know when new stories are posted.

About the story

I was nearing the end of a cardio session and desperately wanting to stop even though I knew I had the physical strength to finish. Desperate to distract myself, I decided to try to focus my thoughts on. The image of a hushed evergreen forest flashed in my mind, intense and vivid. A snow-covered road cut a path through the trees, gently bending leftward out of sight. Along with the image came a thought: *You are walking down a winter road. Do not look ahead. Do not look behind.* In any case, that mental image and those words turned into a story about the power of mindfulness and the expectations that we and others have of ourselves.

A question for the author

Q: What happens when you hit writer's block head on?

A: When I was younger, I experienced a lot of negative self-judgment whenever writer's block struck. I'd gotten it into my head that if I didn't write X number of words every day then I wasn't taking myself seriously. I wasn't a "real" writer, whatever that meant. Thankfully, my feelings on the topic have evolved over time. I've become more accepting of myself, I guess. Basically, if I have the mental energy to write and I'm able to do so, then I do. Sometimes, though, the words refuse to flow or the story refuses to reveal itself. Once, I would have tried to hate myself back to the keyboard and brute force my way through the block. Now, when I get stuck on a particular project, I take a breath and turn my attention to something else. Recently, I've started writing flash fiction as a way to cleanse my creative palate when I encounter writer's block. Because the stories are so short, the stakes feel less weighty, and I'm able to explore and experiment more freely. I like to assign genre categories to the numbers on a 20-sided die and rolling twice. Then, I'll try to write a story based on the genre mashup I've rolled. The creative "play" of the exercise almost always gets me unstuck.

About the author

Katherine Karch spent her childhood playing in the woods, frequently with an old copy of Asimov's or Analog rolled up and tucked in a back pocket. She was still pretty young when she started writing her own stories. For nearly two decades she's continued playing in the woods as a biology teacher. When she's not lesson planning or grading lab reports, she's either reading stories, writing stories, spending time with her family, or sitting quietly in nature, just being. You can find her on Mastodon and Instagram.

www.katherinekarch.com,
@KarchWrites@wandering.shop

A Life of Color

N.V. Haskell

Last fall's decaying leaves shifted beneath my feet as I crossed the yard. The others watched me come, glancing nervously at the infant held tenderly in the old woman's arms. Moonlight flickered through the barren tree branches and glinted off the baby's delicate skin. Her eyes shimmered with rainbows and nebulae beneath eyelashes so pale they were barely visible. It was because of this tiny bundle that I had been hauled from my cozy bed in the middle of the night. What her story was and where she came from were puzzles that I wished hadn't happened on my watch.

The sleep loss fogging my brain faded as I took in the baby's situation. I swore silently, too quietly for any of the three to hear. The old woman had found the baby in the dingy alley behind her home, wrapped in the paint-stained blanket she still wore. The police officer and social worker had come along later. But after David, my boss at the Department of Magical Resources, woke me at 2 am, it became my problem —magic baby, magic expert. It didn't matter that my expertise was adult crimes, not children.

During my last performance appraisal, David had celebrated my departmental loyalty and hinted at a promotion. Using my desire for advancement, he'd easily leveraged me into the weekend rotations by saying it would demonstrate how effectively I could work outside of the crimes division.

Truthfully, the schedule change hadn't been a huge sacrifice. There was nothing for me outside of work. Relationships had proven to be too taxing, not worth the effort I put in. People always left or died, like my parents when I was three. And though the multiple foster homes I'd been raised in had done an adequate job of feeding and housing me, they'd lacked warmth or encouragement. It was no wonder I still sought approval from figures in authority.

Gazing upon the abandoned infant stirred a sympathy for her.

Hard of hearing, the elderly woman had first assumed the cries belonged to the neighborhood cat in heat again. But after the racket persisted for more than an hour, she decided to investigate and phoned the police immediately upon finding the child. The infant was said to be only a few weeks old.

A magical child abandoned was practically unheard of. The magical communities were notoriously private and, although a few of the larger clans had representatives that appeared in governmental regulation meetings when the situation warranted it, most of the smaller clans avoided the greater nonmagical society completely unless they were called on for required services. Several clans had dispersed into unsanctioned areas, which made it difficult for the Department to keep track of them all.

The baby's pale hair and dainty features made her seem angelic, yet beneath her eyelids danced a myriad of colors. With a small, mournful whimper, tears of sapphire blue paint trickled down her face and further stained the blanket. The oil and organic compounds of the paint's pigment mingled with the other smells of the city, the exhaust from the cars and buses, the garbage, and even the odor of the older woman, who rocked the infant gently. She hummed softly, mindless of the streams of colorful goo running from the child's eyes. The woman's toothless smile matched the baby's as she cooed over her. Maybe caring for children came naturally to her.

As the girl drifted peacefully to sleep, her lips puffed slightly with each breath, and I cursed softly again.

Damn David for making me take these weekend on-call shifts. He was well aware that my specialty was magical crimes, not children. I never did well with anything that required special care. A graveyard of dead plants served as proof of my ineptitude; the succulents lasted a bit longer, but ultimately met their demise as well. The moment they came into my possession, their fate was sealed.

I had hoped to be able to pass the baby off quickly, until the social worker thrust a car seat and diaper bag full of supplies at me while informing me that no non-magical homes would take the infant because of her special needs. It fell to my department to find a placement. Although I argued and threatened her with demotion if she left, she flashed a contemptuous look at me before driving away. All I'd be able to do was mention her name in the administrative meeting, come Monday morning.

I knew that finding placement in any home was a challenge, but magical homes were impossible. Their tight-knit communities were scattered in the countryside, sequestered from the curious eyes of nonmagical peoples and understandably hostile to my historically untrustworthy employer. The likelihood of getting help from any of the clans for a child of unknown origin was slim. Though they were fiercely protective of their own, they were unlikely to take in a stray of unusual magical talents. Which made me wonder where the girl had come from.

When David finally answered his phone, he simply told me to 'handle it' and bring the child to the office on Monday morning. He hinted about the promotion I had applied for being a factor. That advancement would remove me from the grunt work and weekend rotations, elevating my footsteps up the corporate ladder as I'd always wanted. It didn't hurt that it came with a hefty pay increase as well.

The task would have been much easier if this were an adolescent or adult of a known clan. The Department's holding cells were constructed to deal with certain magical elements. Soundproof cells for musical clans. Fireproof rooms with automatic extinguishers for the fire clans. Sterile, metal rooms for the nature clans. But there were no facilities for magical children or infants and certainly nothing specifically built for paint magic.

I watched silently as the detective fastened the car seat in the back of my car. Aside from those swirling eyes, the infant appeared just like any other: probably riddled with germs, but also fragile and innocent.

Even though my stomach knotted at the sight of her, I told myself I could manage. I, Laura Arthur, the woman who always declined to hold all her friend's children—was now responsible for taking care of a magical infant for thirty-six hours. Humanity had continued to exist for many thousands of years, right? Certainly, it couldn't be that difficult.

When I got home, I had no choice but to place the baby's car seat beside my bed, which I regretted when she woke up crying and angry three hours later. Anxiety filled me as I tried to figure out how to put an end to the cerulean acrylic streaming from her eyes, or the loud cries erupting from her small lips. A noxious smell, like a mixture of cat pee and stargazer lilies, stung my nostrils as I unclipped the straps that secured her, distracting me from the yellow and green colors that splattered onto my silk pajamas.

When I placed my hands beneath her tiny hips, liquid squished between my fingers. When I pulled my hands away, they were covered in emerald and lemon paint. My disgust was immediate, causing my stomach to churn and threaten emptying. I'd dealt with messes in crime scenes before, but never anything like this. Another sharp wail made me push aside my revulsion. I rushed the car seat, with the still-screaming baby inside it, toward the bathroom.

I placed everything gently in the old clawfoot tub as paint dripped slowly over the sides of the seat. The colors swirled like a kaleidoscope against the white porcelain, blues and reds turning purple and blending with yellow and green to make an ominous hue. There was no time to consider the mess, even though I knew it would take more than bleach to clean it up. I needed help.

I wiped my hands on a towel and, not knowing what else to do, rushed to my neighbor's house. With her one-year-old twins, I considered Molly to be an expert in these matters, and there was no one else that might help. Though we'd only ever said a few polite words here and there, when she saw the distress on my face, she ran back with me. The inside of the bathtub had splotches of bright yellows and oranges from Iris's spittle that dripped in thin ribbons down the white tub's interior.

Loud protests continued as Molly lifted the pink-cheeked girl in her arms and peeled the wet clothes away. The baby was too small to safely bathe in the tub, Molly said. So, we held her in the sink and washed the paint off with a little soap and warm water. The paint swirled down the drain, leaving only traces of orange and blues on the porcelain. The little one's sobs quieted, dissolving into occasional hiccups as we wrapped her in a towel and put a fresh diaper on her.

Molly didn't ask where the baby had come from. She knew where I worked and knew better than to ask questions. Though the paint had obviously surprised her, she had handled it with more grace than I had, and, to her credit, she didn't chide me for not knowing what to do.

An hour after the mess was dealt with, she returned with a bag full of baby items she had intended for donation. She taught me how to prepare formula and test its warmth. I offered to pay her, but she declined and dismissed my apologies, telling me that no one was born knowing what to do.

Eventually the baby dozed off in my arms, and though my limbs ached from holding her for so long, I wasn't sure how to set her down without waking her. When I awoke later, a strand of my hair was tangled in her fingers. She gazed at me with eyes made of swirling sunflower yellow and sunset orange. She let out a low giggle, like she was the only one in on the joke. I couldn't help but smile back, wondering what I looked like to her. Was I swirls of magenta or blotches of grey cast in sharp angles? Maybe I was nothing more than a blurry figure, if she could see me at all.

I shook away those thoughts, reminding myself that it didn't matter anyway. This would only be my problem for one more day. Whatever foster home she wound up in would surely tend to her better than I could.

On Monday morning, I stumbled into the office with my hair in a mess and a streak of neon pink down one shoulder of my houndstooth blouse. One day of diaper disasters and a broken night's sleep had confirmed what I had always known: I wasn't cut out for parenthood.

I'd hoped that by handing the baby off to the Department researchers they could find a link between her and one of the clans catalogued in the database. That should have been the end of my direct involvement, but when David insisted I supervise, that was my day wasted. We didn't get many adults here and no one remembered a child this young ever being brought in. The awareness of the girl's vulnerability in this cold environment put me on edge.

Dr. Arias was gentler with her than I'd expected when he put her through a battery of tests: MRIs, CT scans, EEGs, and EKGs. The lab technicians handled the whimpering baby with a professional detachment while they lined each machine with drop cloths to protect them. It felt as if she were a specimen they were hastily examining in order to classify. Even I thought a baby deserved better than that.

The phlebotomist tried to extract a blood sample with a butterfly needle, but whatever ran through the baby's veins was too thick for the small needle's gauge and using a larger one would be damaging.

Her wails at the needles' prodding made me queasy and brought back old memories of the testing I'd undergone in the foster system when I was small. I remembered feeling alone and afraid. If that testing had shown any magical talents, perhaps I would have had a clan take me in. I hoped that would be the case for this girl.

Iris 15738—her Department-issued name—was special, of that there was no doubt. If she had been from a more prominent clan, the researchers would have quickly lost interest. But because of the rarity of her magic, they wanted to know how it worked and, more importantly, if it could be useful.

In exchange for government aid and certain assurances of land and protections, the magical clans were legally obligated to assist in certain situations. The nature clans handled natural disasters and farming during times of drought. The fire clans were used for controlling burns and military procedures. The musical clans for entertainment and therapy. But the more physically artistic clans were rare. There were only a few sculptors left, and their creations could only animate for a few seconds, which made them practically useless for most purposes.

Years ago, after reforms were passed that gave the clans more autonomy and less oversight, many of the smaller factions had used the new freedom to quietly scatter. After scouring through the Departmental archives, I found only one reference to a paint clan, from decades prior. Address unknown, the phone number attached to them was ancient.

The line crackled when I left a voice message.

Leaving the girl under Dr. Arias' care, I returned to my office to reach out to the small network of approved foster homes with some magical experience. But they each declined. One said they had no room, whereas another honestly said they weren't qualified to handle the babe's issues. I then began the arduous task of calling the larger clans while searching for information about where she might have come from. Then I called a dozen smaller magical settlements within two hundred miles. Eleven had no knowledge of her or her paint magic. The twelfth was the mysterious clan with the ancient number.

David summoned me late in the afternoon, his face somber. Iris slept peacefully in the car seat which was placed in a chair across from his desk.

"Any luck finding a place for her?" he asked, and sighed when I shook my head. "Hate to do this to you, but you'll probably have to keep her for another night or two, unfortunately. We'll cover the damages and I'll add a commendation to your file. Simply fill out the necessary forms and document everything with photographs."

"But—"

"There's no one else, Laura. Jon's got the triplets, and Briana's taking care of her mom. Unless you'd rather give her to the researchers." His lips pursed in disapproval, and he looked away.

We both knew their experiments would turn more invasive without oversight, and Dr. Arias couldn't be there all the time. But there was something else hidden in David's tone.

"What is it?" I asked.

"There's something wrong with her."

My heart sank. Iris stirred in her sleep in the seat next to me. I combed my fingers through her sparse hair and waited for him to continue.

"Her brain activity is abnormal, probably due to hydrocephalus, or whatever it's called with paint." He paused, trying to make sure that I couldn't misunderstand. "Her heart is arrhythmic, most likely working too hard to pump the thick fluid around her body, but without testing her enzymes we can't be sure. There's no cure."

Iris's chest rose and fell, accompanied by an occasional pause or gasp. Petite hands clutched the edges of a pink blanket. It was probably Dr. Arias who had placed a plush giraffe beside her, its head was already covered in mint green acrylic drool. It reminded me of the stuffed horse I'd been given in my first foster home. I'd carried it with me through a dozen other homes, a source of security and something soft to hold in an otherwise hard world.

"Dr. Arias doesn't think she'll make it past a year," David said. He looked at me warily, as if I were going to fall apart at the news.

I tried to keep my expression neutral and steady the sudden throb in my heart. After everything she'd been through in her short life, the girl didn't deserve this fate. Iris deserved to live. I took a deep breath. "Percentages?"

"Eighty percent chance she has a stroke, heart attack, or turns septic in the next six months. One hundred percent within the next year."

My chest deflated as ideas for a solution rushed through my mind. "But if we find where she came from, there might be a chance."

David shrugged. "Only if you can find her clan and convince them to talk to us."

By the end of the first week, I'd resorted to wearing shapeless, faded clothing once reserved for yard work or donation The days were whirlwinds of endless feedings, diapers, and departmental meetings. The sleepless nights left me in a dazed stupor. My home's modern décor had turned into a canvas splashed with bright acrylics and oils. But aside from the damage being done, there were growing smiles and curious hands that slowly tugged at my emotional armor as Iris planted something both unfamiliar and uncomfortably vulnerable beneath it.

There was still no home willing to take her, not once the Department revealed her complications, but the thought of leaving her with the researchers made me nauseous. Adults who committed magic-based crimes were all dealt with properly; I'd made sure of it because I understood how the judicial system worked in those cases. And although the Department of Magical Resources had gone to great lengths to make amends for its past through media outlets and charity initiatives, most everyone suspected they kept certain practices covert.

Without an advocate, Iris might disappear within a month. Though I'd never witnessed anything personally, there were long-standing rumors about experimentation that occurred in the Department's mysterious lower levels. I'd thought that it was all conjecture, but now the fear that there might be truth to it worried me. Iris was more vulnerable than I'd ever been.

The ambitious governmental loyalist that I'd always been began to question everything, including why my other assignments were becoming less important to me when compared to Iris.

In desperation, I reached out again to the magical communities, widening the radius to five hundred miles—with the same sad result. According to one trusted magical resource, the paint clans had vanished years ago. No one knew anything about Iris and after a few brief questions, no one wanted her, either. Despite the Department's considerable resources and informants, we had yet to reach the one elusive clan. But I left another message on their nondescript voicemail and waited.

The following weeks felt like an eternity. My coworkers had been helping with feedings and diaper changes during work hours, but something strange began to happen. Iris would scream hysterically until returned to my arms. Briana nearly dropped the struggling girl when she attempted to change her. And the Department was having to reimburse not only my costs, but many of my coworkers' wardrobes after Iris's messy cries and accidents. With each feeding and diaper change, my coworkers were met with Iris's growing levels of hysteria, until they stopped offering to help altogether. And as Iris's cries grew louder, a subtle pressure began to grow around me. One email complained that Iris was upsetting the office's routine and productivity. Another suggested that if we couldn't find a home for her, the researchers on level 3-B would be happy to study her until she passed away. Level 3-B's enthusiasm at gaining more information about paint magic by studying an ill child was off-putting, to say the least.

David's behavior changed drastically over the same time frame. Where he'd initially insisted that I keep Iris and shown concern for her wellbeing, his tone changed to annoyance bordering on disdain. More than once, he suggested that I consider leaving her at the facility overnight so that I could get a full night's rest, but I heard the veiled demand in his voice. I suspected that the change was the result of pressure from his superiors. When I continued to resist, David asked that I stay away from meetings so that Iris didn't cause a distraction. In fact, I was encouraged to work from home, but refused. I watched helplessly as projects I was vying for were given to less qualified coworkers. Knowing I risked my promotion, I swallowed my anger and frustration, though I wrote down every detail of what was happening.

All hope of finding Iris' clan began to fade away.

One afternoon, David's tall figure filled the doorway of my office, a room now spotted teal and lemon, with the lingering scent of hydrocarbons hanging in the air. His carefully crafted appearance of morality was slipping away with each of our interactions.

"I can practically guarantee that promotion if you will give her up, Laura." His gaze never left mine as he spoke. "The Regional Director is offering a significant raise, too. I'm sure you must be exhausted from dealing with her. Give her to the Department, and rest assured that they will take care of her for the rest of her days."

I sighed and rubbed my eyes, silently begging for the headache that had been etched behind them for the past few weeks to ease up temporarily. For a fleeting second, I considered giving in. But I'd been a child in the system once and Iris deserved no less than what I'd had. A warm bed, a gentle word, patience. David's assurances rang hollow and while caring for her didn't feel quite as overwhelming as it once had, the thought of leaving her alone and afraid made me ill. Iris needed me and maybe I'd needed her to remind me that there was a life outside of work.

"You're okay with her disappearing into the system?" I asked.

David winced at the contempt in my voice while I studied the green and blue staining in the creases of my hands. In the process of giving up rest, personal care, and anything resembling normalcy for the past six weeks, I'd realized that there were some things I couldn't in good conscience do. Even if it was for the agency. I had come too far with Iris to back out now. Fuck him and the Department for asking me to. His face hardened as I said as much. He walked away, taking my advancement with him as Iris began to cry.

My cell phone vibrated at 3 am a week later. I rushed to answer it before it disturbed Iris, scurrying into the living room, now painted in sporadic shades of Tahitian blue, lilac, and burnt sienna.

"Did you call about a baby?" an older woman whispered over the connection.

My voice wavered as I answered, "Yes." Anticipation swelled within me, hoping this was the call I'd been waiting for. "I'm Laura Arthur from the Department of—"

"Don't say it," she snapped. "Tell me what she looks like."

"The baby?"

She took a deep, shuddering breath, filled with emotional restraint.

Flippant words that all babies looked alike nearly left my mouth. But that was old thinking and now felt completely disingenuous. An awkward tension stretched in the silence between us. That she was calling at this time of night with a lowered voice led me to the conclusion that she was afraid of being discovered. Our time was limited. "Blonde hair, round face, colorful, swirling eyes—like they're full of..."

"Paint." Her voice was heavy and raw. "I'll give you an address. Meet me there tomorrow at one pm. I need to see her."

I jotted down the location and the line went dead before I had a chance to ask any more questions. When I returned to the bedroom, Iris had wriggled from one side of her crib to the other, leaving a long squiggle of avocado green behind her. I didn't bother telling David why I wouldn't be coming into work that Thursday and he didn't care enough to ask anyway.

It was a two-hour drive from my home, through the suburbs and into the stark rural countryside. We travelled past fields and small clusters of ramshackle homes set far off the road, many partially hidden behind enchanted conifers and hedges that moved to protect the view of the settlements as I passed.

The address the woman had given directed me to an abandoned gas station, a dilapidated relic of a bygone era. The weather-beaten windows were glazed and cracked and worn chunks of concrete were interspersed with layers of indiscernible graffiti. Generations of spiders nourished themselves on fat insects in all corners of the building. As I pulled my vehicle into the weedy vacant lot, a faint silhouette shifted behind the chipped double doors.

With one hand tucked under the carrier and the other gripping a bag filled with baby supplies and a crusted giraffe, I hesitantly stepped towards the entrance. Hope and dread bloomed equally inside me.

The door groaned in protest as I pushed it open, revealing an interior cloaked in a thick fog of dust motes that were illuminated through narrow shafts of sunlight.

A tall woman stood in the back of the room, her wrinkles betraying her age, and her bright red hair pulled tightly in a bun. Her eyes were made of varied colors that swirled together. She fingered a necklace of glass beads looped around her throat. Most were painted in vibrant colors, but one was plain, as if something were missing.

Fear and reticence filled the air between us, neither of us willing to take a step forward. The woman's eyes darted towards the carrier when Iris moved inside. Her lips quivered.

"May I see her?" she asked softly.

I set the carrier on the floor and pulled down the soft blanket. I cradled Iris in my arms, hesitating. It'd been a long time since anyone else had held her.

"Who are you?" I asked.

"Messina Thawn, of clan Thawn. I'm surprised you found us." Gently, she drew Iris into her arms and swayed from one foot to the other in the rocking motion most parents seemed to know instinctively. A sad smile pulled at her lips. "I'm sorry for making you wait for a response. That number you had is old, set up ages ago for emergencies when our last leader was alive. It's rarely checked; our current clan leader is stricter, doesn't believe in using technology under any circumstances. Not even when it could bring one of our missing back to us." She paused to brush the hair from Iris's forehead. "We've managed to mostly avoid the Department's notice for decades. Ever since their experiments ended back in the thirties." Her look dared me to respond. "I bet they don't teach that in school anymore."

I shifted uncomfortably, understanding what she avoided saying and that reaching out and meeting me was a risk for her. I cleared my throat. "Does she have a name?"

She shook her head, gazing again at Iris. "I wouldn't know it. Gabby, my daughter, ran away when she discovered she was pregnant. Left with a farm boy." Her voice hitched. "I looked for her. We all did. But she was afraid of what would happen. Not everyone in our clan is accepting of the nonmagical mix. They probably thought they'd do better in the city."

Affection swept across Messina's face, but her smile faded into barely suppressed grief. "I knew something had gone wrong. I felt it. As if she'd drunk turpentine and faded away." She sniffed, tried to collect herself before she continued. "Leo, the boy, returned a few weeks ago. He's refused to talk to any of us. Won't even say what happened or where my Gabby dissolved. I can't even add her bead to my necklace."

"Bead?" I asked.

"It's the only thing we leave behind when we die." Messina cleared her throat to cover the tremor in her voice. "A bead coated with our colors."

Iris stirred in her arms, squirming her shoulders against her grandmother's bony chest. Her lashes fluttered open, seeing eyes like her own. Similar, but not the same. It was easier to see the differences when they were so close. One was orderly lines; the other was blurring chaos.

Messina gasped. Blood-red tears welled in her eyes. "Oh, no." It was a soft sound, like whispering down a moss-ridden well.

"The researchers said she was sick. But I thought her clan might be able to help." I choked on the question. "Was I... am I wrong?"

Messina's breath shuddered. Painted tears trickled down her cheeks as Iris's small fingers brushed at them curiously before tangling in the glass beads around Messina's neck.

"There's a recessive gene that runs in our clan. It keeps some of us from solidifying completely. Bones that can't harden turn to mush. The lining of organs and blood vessels eventually breaks down until our colors run together. Dissolving little by little. I hoped that Leo's influence would override..." Her words were knives cutting us both.

"Can't you help her? What about the rest of the clan? There must be someone." At the sudden rise of my voice, Iris turned. Small arms reached for me as she whimpered.

Mindless of the violet paint that splattered the front of her dress, Messina cradled the girl to her chest for a moment and sighed. She shook her head, eyes holding endless depths of anguish as she returned Iris to me.

"One of my sisters died before she was one. My nephew was the same. There's nothing anyone can do." Her fingers glided from one bead to the next before she stroked the back of Iris's head. "All you can do is care for her until she passes."

"Me? She's your family. Surely, you'd want to keep her."

"No one knows I'm here," she said, her voice gone low. The palm she pressed to her lips was covered in Iris's violet paint. Messina closed her eyes for a long moment. As her hand slowly dropped, a bright smear stained her lips and chin. "If she'd been born amongst our clan with that anomaly, she would have been dissolved already. Her life would have been shorter than in your care. Maybe even shorter than with your researchers."

"But I thought the clans... I thought that you took care of your own."

"Laura, even if we were a stronger clan with more resources, nothing could stop what is happening to her. All we have is our limited magic, and after watching so many of our children die over the years, we try to lessen the suffering." Her tears welled again. "If you want her to live a bit longer, it's best she stays with you. Plus, she's already bonded to you."

"I can't care for her. I don't know how to do *any* of this." My voice trembled, and I quelled the volume to keep from upsetting Iris further.

Messina brushed my hair from my cheek with stained fingers. "What do you need to know? Feed her when she's hungry, clean her when she's dirty, bathe her, soothe her, and hold her."

I whispered, "I can't watch her die."

Something within me broke; the veneer of strength I relied on splintered and cascaded down my cheeks. I hadn't let myself cry in a long time. So long that I'd nearly forgotten the initial sting and briny taste of my tears. Messina wiped my cheeks with gentle hands, studying the clear liquid on her fingertips before looking back at me sympathetically.

"Life and love are messy and fragile. No matter how much of either you have, it won't ever prepare you for when you have to let go." She enveloped us in her slender arms, painting my cheek with her sorrow.

Messina said a quiet goodbye as she helped place the girl in the car, stroking her face one last time with tenderness and grief.

My gaze lingered on her necklace as words stuck in my throat. "When she... her bead..."

"Keep it," she said. "It's clan tradition to wear it when someone you love passes away. It will give you something to hold when she's gone. Something to remember the colors of her life with."

Other than pulling over twice to collect myself, I remember little of the drive home. Leaving the dusty gas station, I'd vowed to protect Iris until her very last breath. No matter how much her paint stained my clothing, furniture, and skin, it was a small price to pay to hear her full-belly chortles and breathe in her sweet-smelling hair.

The following day, I found myself in a tense talk with David as I put in my request for a leave of absence and demanded payout for my untaken paid time off and the standard payment for foster parents. Our meeting then transitioned into an extensive virtual conference with the district manager and head researchers. When they attempted to bribe or threaten me, I responded with promises to publicize our exchanges and involve contacts above their heads. I hoped they didn't catch the tremor in my voice. It was half lying, of course, but I refused to abandon this lost child the way everyone else had. The meeting resulted in an extended leave of absence and veiled promises of professional stagnation.

The green and gold of summer were giving way to dusky autumn when Iris finally rolled over. A few weeks later, she discovered her feet whilst gurgling happily on her back. Her peals of laughter shook the house intermittently for days. A month later, Molly and the twins were visiting when Iris sat up on her own for the first time. Molly had become my confidant and biggest asset for all the things I didn't know about babies. She celebrated each milestone with me and stroked my back in my moments of frailty.

Soon after, Iris scooted across the floor for the first time. I no longer minded the dapples of orange and sapphire that seeped between the grooves of the oak planks. Everything could be cleaned or replaced someday.

She delighted in the tastes of pureed peaches and sweet potatoes and claimed a stuffed parrot as a new favorite toy. At eight months—just when I'd hit the depths of sleep-deprived despair—she began to sleep through the night consistently. I focused on celebrating each small milestone as if it were a miracle. Because each breath she took, every smile, each drop of paint—everything she did and each moment we shared—was miraculous to me. I hadn't known it was possible to love like this, knowing it would end.

Iris's attempts to pull herself up were weak, her body unable to coordinate the movement, and each time I raised her to her feet in an attempt to stand, her knees would buckle like a dropped scarf. It was a bleak winter day when fear humbled me enough to reach out to Dr. Arias. He was kind in his response and, under the guise of research, he began to visit us weekly and provide some guidance with her care.

"Her muscles are beginning to atrophy." His voice was strained. He stroked her head gently, his cold professional demeanor dissolved into warmth at the sight of Iris's smile. "Maybe another month or two at most."

It took a long moment for my words to form. "Is she hurting?"

He shook his head. "Not yet. I can prescribe something if you want...just to keep her comfortable."

Iris never spoke in words, but I learned her language of cries and grunts. When I accidentally stepped on toys I'd forgotten to pick up, I didn't curse them. The pain of my body was a temporary distraction to the deeper rending inside me.

I'd never had faith in anything other than science, but there were days of mounting desperation when I found myself standing beside her crib while she slept, and I prayed in the same way one of my foster parents had. Sometimes I would rub the smooth glass bead strung around my neck repeatedly, as if some divine force would notice my plea and take pity. But whomever, or whatever, I prayed to, never answered.

When daffodils broke through the cold ground outside my windows and spring ushered in new signs of life, I'd known for days what was happening. And yet I wasn't ready. I don't imagine I ever would have been.

I'd been steadily increasing her pain medication to make her passing easier. But as I cradled her frail frame against my chest, I felt a weight of sorrow that no amount of preparation could have lightened.

I breathed in Iris's familiar scent. The warmth of her body soothed me as I tried to comfort her. The colors of her eyes dimmed, the slow swirling stilled. Her lips trembled in her final breaths as her tiny frame shuddered. I whispered words of love, fighting back my tears so that the last thing she saw on my face wouldn't be my sorrow. I only wanted her to know my love. There would be time to grieve for years to come.

Her occasional gasps lessened. The rise and fall of her chest eventually stopped. Iris slipped away in a final swirl of sunflower yellow and sapphire blues as she dissolved in my arms.

All that was left of her was a bead painted with beauty and love.

See N.V. Haskell's story "A Life of Color" online at Metaphorosis.
If you liked it, leave a comment. Authors love that!
Remember to subscribe to our e-mail updates so you'll know when new stories are posted.

About the story

I thought about this story for years before I had the courage to write it and I am grateful for the right editor who encouraged me to expand it to what it has become.

Coming from a troubled childhood, I convinced myself that I would never have children. Consequently, when I became pregnant in my early twenties I was overwhelmed with conflicting emotions and had very little support or resources. When I lost that pregnancy, I was devastated. But if I hadn't had that experience and gotten the help that I needed afterward, I'm not sure that I would have had my family or be the person I am today. Although it was a life-altering combination of humbling and heartbreaking, it made me realize that, until then, I'd had no idea what I wanted. It completely changed my perspective and ultimately made me work to become a better person.

Over the last few years, a few friends have suffered miscarriages. Another lost a young child. Grieving with them compelled me to finally write this story.

Although it was many years ago, and my children are now grown, I still occasionally think about the child that might have been. I wonder what kind of magic they might have brought to this world, and, at the same time, I am grateful for the gift they gave me. I only wish that I had something more than words to hold on to.

A question for the author

Q: Do you use critique groups or other resources to polish your writing?

A: I am in three writing groups on Discord with writers at all levels of experience. We regularly trade stories, and the feedback and perspectives of others has been instrumental to my growth as a writer. Plus, after reading other people's work and critiquing it, then seeing them incorporate that feedback to improve a storyline or fill in a plot hole feels great. For instance, one of the smaller groups I am in (there's only five of us) took one person's story and gave deep feedback on what worked and what wasn't clear. That story ended up winning a major writing competition and we celebrated with him when he picked up his award.

I also rely on a couple of beta readers who consistently read over 100 books a year and provide great reactions and questions strictly from a reader perspective. The issues they bring up are often quite different from the writers and provide some interesting insight into how that piece is perceived and whether I hit the mark.

About the author

N.V. Haskell is an award-winning author of speculative fiction who lives somewhere between civilization and the haunted caves of Kentucky with her long-suffering spouse, rescue pets, and too many squirrels and groundhogs that she can't help but feed.

When she's not busy writing, you can find her attending Comic Cons or Renaissance Fairs donned in her favorite costumes, running badly, or trying to read too many books at a time. After many years in healthcare, she remains stubbornly (or foolishly) optimistic.

www.nvhaskell.com, @NhHaskell

The Bookseller of Mars

Gaby Brogan

I am where the hurt people go. Not the crying, soft, gentle people. I'm not sure there are any of those left. No, I am where the killers turn when the buried piece of them that is still human reaches out, yearning for the light.

Now there are two killers at my door. Boy-children. I see them on the crackly intercom screen in my kitchen, the red desert stretching out behind them. I will let them in, I'm sure. I always do.

"Guns stay outside," I call through the mic.

They turn to each other and whisper. They look about fourteen or fifteen – the age I was when I first came to Mars over a decade ago, a filthy, scared teenage girl, bundled onto a starship along with the rest of the refugees from Earth.

Originally, thirty thousand of the global elite were planned for those starships. But when society fell to floods, fire, and disease, SpaceCorp took whoever could make it to the launch site in burning California. Beggars can't be choosers during the apocalypse.

The day we landed, I filed out of the ship into the sterile light of the Mars station with the other aching, stinking survivors. We took gear from metal boxes as an armed group of SpaceCorp employees watched over us. The most precious item was a metal cube the size of my fist. If I pressed the button, it would pop open to the size of a cargo container. A ready-made home for the elite's life on Mars; temperature controlled, CO_2 to oxygen conversion, a greenhouse for food, and a drillbug to bore down into Martian rock for water.

That cargo container is where I find myself now, all these years later. Hidden under an outcrop of rock on the edge of the desert, far from the violence and squalor of the settlements.

"We're not leaving our gun," calls the blond kid on my screen.

"Then you aren't coming in." On Mars, everyone's a killer.

The kid kicks the ground, sending up a cloud of ochre dust.

"You don't understand. It's Jay," he gestures to the boy next to him. "His regulator's beeping."

"I'm sorry," I say. "That's a real problem for Jay." If his regulator is beeping, he doesn't have long. That vital metal chip sits in your nostril, creating a bubble of oxygen and pressure that stops your blood from boiling in the Martian atmosphere. Beeping means breaking.

"Fuck," says the blond. He turns to Jay and motions to put the gun on the ground. Jay shakes his head and grips it tighter.

I move a plant's green tendril to hit the intercom button again. "I'm alone here, if it makes you feel better. And I don't have a gun... within easy reach." I look at the stack of books next to my bed. A pistol sits on top.

The blond grabs Jay's shoulders, pleading, but the other boy simply stares into the intercom camera and holds the gun to his chest.

He'd rather die than come into my house unarmed? Jesus. Who knows what they've been through.

I groan. This kid is about to die on my doorstep because of his own stubbornness. I've buried bodies in the rocky ground before, but none this young.

Pushing the button, I open my cargo container's airlock. The boys whip their heads around and scramble in, the door slamming down after them. It floods with air and repressurizes.

On my airlock monitor, I see Jay breathing deeply. Tears stream down the blond's cheeks through the red dust. He scoops Jay into a ferocious hug, gripping his silver jacket so hard I think it might rip.

The kids hold each other like that until I press the button to open the door to my home. They separate, tense and defensive, hurt wolf pups ready to bite. Jay raises the gun, but his hands are shaky, uncertain.

"That was pretty fucking stupid," I say. "Put the gun down. I'm not going to hurt you."

The blond wipes his tears. Jay lowers the gun. That's better.

Martian-born kids. They're slimmer, muscles softer than mine were, growing up on Earth. They walk with a graceful float in their step, no muscle memory of Earth's gravity weighing down their every move. They remind me of birds – hollow bones.

Jay is short, on the childish side of his teen years, with red-brown skin like the Martian dust. His eyes are honey. His blond friend is so pale I can see his blue veins. He's taller than Jay and his wide eyes dart around my home.

I gesture for them to sit at the scrap-metal table. They do, and Jay lays the gun by his feet.

"I'm Melanie. Tea?"

"Uh, yes please," says the blond. "I'm Ben."

I busy myself over at the sink, filling a pot with water and setting it on the thermal pad to heat.

"So, what are two kids doing out in the Martian desert with a failing regulator?" I scoop dried herbs into three mesh metal balls and set each in a mug.

"Got lost on a school trip," says Ben. "We were trying to walk back to our settlement when the beeping started. *Bookseller* is the only thing on the map in this part of the desert. We knew you were our only hope for getting air."

I snort. "I didn't know I was a feature on any maps." Maps of Mars are rarely accurate, anyway, often scrawled on wheat husk paper after a long journey. But if these boys go to school, it means they're from the SpaceCorp settlement – the only place with the resources to build any real infrastructure. The most organized settlement we have. And the most vicious. Perhaps they have half-decent maps. What they definitely don't have, however, is school trips. These boys are liars. And most likely, runaways. "Aren't you lucky you managed to find me."

I feel the cold tip of a gun at my back. Damn.

"Why'd you tell us you were alone?" asks Jay. "I see two plates stacked up there on your drying rack. Two cups. Two forks. You got a boyfriend hiding here?"

I flick a look at my drying rack.

"Girlfriend," I say. "And no. She's gone. Just a few days ago... I – I didn't have the heart to put it all away yet, if you must know."

On Mars, you get used to reading the truth in someone's voice. I guess he hears mine.

"Oh." The gun moves away from my back.

"She isn't dead." I can't stand for this kid's sympathy to be wasted on the idea of Cara. "Just gone. Apparently, life in a settlement is more interesting than here surrounded by badly written books." I slam the teas down and slump into my seat. Jay and Ben watch me warily. "Now, if you're quite done threatening me, maybe we can enjoy this tea."

Ben kicks Jay under the table. "Uh, yeah. Sorry," Jay manages.

"So... uh, you make all this yourself?" Ben gestures around my cargo container home. Masters of conversation, these two.

I look around. He doesn't mean the greenhouse extension, the shelves, or the tins of preserved foods, which, as a matter of fact, I did make myself. He means the towers of books that line every wall.

"They don't call me the bookseller for nothing," I shrug.

"How'd you do all this?" A spark of wonder lights Ben's blue eyes. Now, even in my lonely, heartbroken state, I'm not going to destroy what might be the only spark of wonder currently on Mars.

I sigh. "After the starships landed, everyone in the settlements started acting out the sequel to the earthly apocalypse — real Mad Max shit. I ran out here into the desert alone and popped my cargo container. Raised myself until I got an infected cut and had to venture back into a settlement to trade my food for medicine. While I was there, I met a guy who'd pulp wheat husks and turn it into paper. I came back and traded all my preserves for five notebooks."

"That's a bad trade," says Ben.

"I know," I snort. "But I wasn't in the healthiest state of mind. Anyway, I started by re-writing the classics, from memory, as well as I could. Everything I'd been studying in school on Earth. Some part of me knew they were worth saving and I'm glad I did. They sold first when I went back to the settlement to trade. Then, people started visiting me, threatening me, demanding I write the books they'd left behind. Soon, they realized they'd get better stories if they were kinder. Creativity can't exactly flourish at gunpoint."

They'd wanted the stories so desperately. You see, when your home is burning or filled with your dying family, you don't think to bring your favorite book or e-reader as you escape. You just get your weapon and get yourself to the launch site by any means necessary. And on Mars, there's no infrastructure to build phones or TVs. Our exodus from Earth meant we left all our stories behind.

"People told me plots and I spun them into books. And now, that's all I do, rewriting shittier versions of the books we had on Earth."

"And it's safe here?" asks Ben. "Settlers don't ever raid you?"

"I rewrote *The Handmaid's Tale* for the leader of a raider gang a while back. It's been particularly quiet since then. Maybe she put in a good word for me."

I sip my tea. Indeed, my customers are hard, bitter people. Did you ever see those pictures of a fox or a crocodile or a bear — some creature that is all claws and bite — with a butterfly landing on their nose? They used to put those pictures in cheap yearly calendars. Anyways, the biter closes their eyes and they let the butterfly land, because behind the claws there's a soft warm creature that just wants a nap in the sun. In my little cargo container, killers rest and tell me about their favourite books. They ask me to write a story. And I do, because sometimes, I see the horror and the haunt slip away. Just for a moment.

"So basically, you just hide out here and sell stories to the dangerous assholes who come through?" asks Jay.

"I —" Ouch. "Better than being stranded in the desert on a school trip... or are you running away from SpaceCorp?"

Jay's hand drifts down to his gun.

"Hands where I can see them. Or I won't be fixing that regulator of yours."

His hand shoots back to his lap. "You can fix it?"

I nod. "Put your gun up there, next to mine. On top of that stack of books."

Jay waits for a consenting look from Ben and then stands, placing the gun next to mine.

"Much better. Now, give me your regulator."

He fishes it out of his nose, wipes it on his trousers, and sets it on the table.

"Right, I'll get to it. You guys can wait over there," I gesture to the pile of pillows and blankets that serves as my sofa. I tell them they can help themselves to whatever food or books they want, as long as they're quiet.

They busy themselves raiding my shelves. Ben munches on some dried carrot chips I made last week. Jay stares out the kitchen window at the endless red ocean.

I open my box of tools, grab the magnifying glass, and get to work. But a few minutes in, I lean back in my chair.

"Who made this regulator?" I ask.

"Does it matter?" Jay snaps.

"Kind of. It's a piece of shit."

It's more than that. This regulator isn't like the one I took from the SpaceCorp boxes when I landed, built to last a lifetime. It's flimsy, designed to break after a few days. Why would anyone make this? Nothing on Mars is disposable. Every scrap we have is precious, used carefully, made for a reason. Sending someone out with this is a death sentence.

"Can you fix it, though?" asks Jay.

"I don't know. It's going to take me a little longer."

Ben sat up. "How much longer? We uh... we need to get moving soon."

"Why? Someone coming after you?"

He looks at the carrot chips in his hand.

"Fine, don't tell me. But I need at least a day or two on this."

"Shit."

"Up to you."

The boys whisper to each other in the corner.

"We can't pay you for fixing the regulator. Or for letting us stay while we do," says Jay, finally.

"Oh." On Mars, nothing is free. "Then you can help out here – the greenhouse needs fixing up and I've been meaning to repair the shelves."

The boys nod, relieved. I set them up with their tasks and then spend a few hours tinkering with the regulator. In the evening, I warm up some soup for dinner and they sit on the blankets, flipping through my handwritten books and asking questions. It feels good to speak to someone, again.

The next morning, I go back to work on the regulator. The Martian time slips by, quiet and red.

"*To Kill a Mockingbird*?" asks Ben, in the afternoon. "What is it, like a guide?"

"Sure, it's a guide. But not one to do with birds," I say. Jay looks up from the old drillbug he's trying to fix.

"I don't get it," says Ben.

"Sit and read it and you will," I say.

"It's long."

"Ah but it's worth it. Books are more nourishing than you know."

Jay and Ben share a look — a hint of a laugh, a twist of embarrassment on my behalf. Not quite an eye roll, but nearly. I smile. My little brother and I shared that exact look about the nearest clueless adult countless times. He didn't make it past the first wave of sickness back on Earth.

I shake my head. "Take it."

Ben's eyebrows shoot up and he looks at Jay. Jay smiles.

"Well, thanks." Ben holds it gentler now, flipping softly through the pages.

That book is worth three weeks of food in a trade. I can practically see Cara in the corner, chastising me about economic irresponsibility. Well, she isn't here.

Ben reads my rehashed version of *To Kill a Mockingbird* and I watch him out of the corner of my eye. It's one of the few books with words I know I've written right. The lady who commissioned the first copy had the text tattooed on her shoulder, "*I wanted you to see what real courage is, instead of getting the idea that courage is a man with a gun in his hand. It's when you know you're licked before you begin, but you begin anyway and see it through no matter what.*"

I always liked that quote.

The next day, the intercom buzzes like a yellowjacket. I flick a look toward the screen.

Now, these are the kind of guests I'm used to. A man and a woman stand tall, decked out in cobbled-together desert-gear and heavy-duty boots. Their faces are obscured by rags. Guns hang from their shoulders and grenades from their belts. Raiders or SpaceCorp, I can't tell. All the same, anyway — grizzly bears.

"Good morning," I say over the intercom. "You've reached the bookseller."

"You seen two boys out here?"

"Hard to say. Who are you?"

"Retrievers, from the SpaceCorp school. Those two students killed a member of staff and ran away. We've come to ensure they receive proper punishment."

Shit. I take my hand off the intercom and spin toward Ben and Jay.

"Is that true?" I don't want trouble.

Ben shakes his head. Jay nods.

"We each killed a guy," says Jay. He talks fast like he can see I'm spooked. "But they made us, as part of our training. That's why we ran away."

"Training?"

"It's not a school. They're training kids as soldiers and planning to take over the other settlements by force and form a proper country, led by them. They haven't come to punish us. They want to stop the truth getting out before they're ready."

This is huge. Finally making the settlements into one city, united, makes sense. Resources could be shared. A society could be built. Well, that's what logic says. In practice, the one settlement that SpaceCorp already runs is brutal, with settlers fighting over scraps from the people at the top. A takeover is going to be violent. And bloody.

The intercom buzzes again.

"Bookseller," says the man on the intercom. "Did you see the boys?"

I press the mic. Ben's hand twitches on *To Kill a Mockingbird.*

"Yes," I say. "I have seen the boys." Jay scrambles to grab his gun. "They passed through here a few days ago and left. Said they were heading to the northern settlement. One of them had a broken regulator. I doubt they'll have made it far."

The man and woman nod. This is no surprise to them. They know those regulators don't last.

"So you just let them go?" says the woman.

"Obviously. I don't need two more mouths to feed. If they want to get themselves killed in the desert, that's on them."

The man and woman scuff around in the dust, whispering to one another.

"On behalf of SpaceCorp, we're requesting entry to your home, bookseller. To trade for supplies," says the man.

"I've got nothing to trade but books."

"That'll do."

He's clearly not coming in for books.

I consider my options.

"Guns stay outside. That's my policy."

On the little screen, the man nods and hands his gun to the woman. She takes a few steps back, looking at the perimeter of my house. No doubt making sure no figures escape as her colleague searches inside.

Behind me, Ben and Jay's panicked whispers fill the air. I usher them under my bed and pass them my pistol. Their wide-eyed faces disappear as I throw a blanket over the bed.

Pushing the button, I open the airlock and the man walks in. It repressurizes.

It's not ideal. If he finds them, then what? Can I feasibly say that I didn't know they were there?

Another press of a button and the man is in my home. He lowers his mouth rag. His face is pitted and scarred, like the surface of our new home.

"I'll take a look around now," he says. He's done us both a favor by dropping the pretense.

"Go ahead," I say.

He walks along the towers of books, and I look at my home of over a decade with fresh eyes. Not many hiding spots. The bed is glaringly obvious.

The man drops to his knees to check out the entrance to the greenhouse. He stands and cocks his head, reading the spine of a book on a precarious stack. My rendition of *The Catcher in the Rye*.

"Interested?" I ask.

"No," he says. "I've heard your prices. I'm not in the market to waste three weeks' worth of food on a book." His eyes linger on it, though.

"Well, they take me a long time to write. You read this one back on Earth?"

"Uh, yeah. As a matter of fact, I did."

"Go on then, what did you do, before? Office guy?"

He considers me. "I was a teacher in New York," he says, finally. "Math. Always liked that book, though."

"Bet it's a bit different now, working at SpaceCorp."

His face clouds over and he looks away. Wrong thing to say. Don't remind killers of what they are. I've become too used to the truthful simplicity of my conversations with the boys. This feels like a deadly chess match that I'm being forced to play once again.

His eyes catch on the three mugs in that damn drying rack. The plates. He sighs and walks towards the bed.

"Don't you miss stories?" I ask.

He turns back. "Let me just get this over with, lady."

I ignore him. "There's no TV here. No cinema. I think that's why people like my books. Medicine for the mind – a way to get lost.”

He blinks. More people need a mental escape on Mars than they're willing to admit.

“If only there were a way for you to procure a story without having to trade your hard-earned food.”

I take *Catcher in the Rye* off the stack of books and hold it out to him.

His face is a mirror-image of Ben's when I gave him *To Kill a Mockingbird*. On Mars, you only own what you need to survive.

Slowly, he reaches out to take the book. He holds it in both hands, eyes roving over Cara's illustration of the cover. It's beautiful, like everything else she created. He flips open the first page, gently.

“So... have you found what you're looking for?”

“Perhaps.”

His eyes flick to the bed again. What's the price for two kids' lives?

“Take another,” I say. “For the road.”

He spins around and looks at the stack of books next to him. *Percy Jackson and The Olympians.* He pulls it out quickly and stuffs both books into the inside of his jacket pocket.

"My students used to love Percy Jackson," he says. "Back on Earth."

That's the thing about my sanctuary – even killers have an inner child. And stories help them find their way back out.

"I bet," I say and indicate the airlock.

He nods. I push the button and he walks out into the Martian desert.

I rush to the intercom screen. Outside, he gestures, talking to his colleague. She questions him. He shrugs. She tips her head, and they kick around in the dust for a while. Then, they turn and go.

My hands are shaking, white.

"You can come out," I say.

The boys scramble out from under the bed. Ben runs at me and hugs me. Jay hovers behind. "Thank you," he says.

Ben lets me go and I exhale all the tension.

To think, Cara left because of how quiet life was here with me, how slow.

We collapse at the table.

"So, you guys ran away from SpaceCorp. No destination in mind?"

"Not exactly," says Jay. "A few weeks ago, these girls from the year above broke into the SpaceCorp offices. They read through a bunch of documents. Plans for the new country, breakthroughs in terraforming. The girls stole the papers and a bunch of supplies then ran away to start a new settlement. A hidden one for Martian kids, where we can try to build something better."

"And you're going to follow them. How do you know their regulators didn't break?"

"These girls are smart. Their regulators didn't break."

"Do you even know where they are?"

"They've gone to the western mountain." Jay's face looks young, hopeful.

I consider these two Martian kids. They aren't killers. They don't have claws and fangs. Maybe they're the butterflies on the predator's nose. Or I'm confusing my metaphors; I said they were hollow-boned birds, right? Either way. They are a thing with wings. And they see a future on Mars, one away from the suffering and the violence.

"Well, then I'd best get that regulator fixed up for you," I say.

The boys spend the evening browsing my shelves while I tinker and process the impending doom of a SpaceCorp takeover.

An unfamiliar noise fills my home. I look up. It's the boys, laughing. They're reading bits of a book to one another, acting out scenes with big, exaggerated movements. I tilt my head. *The Hitchiker's Guide to the Galaxy*. How strange, to hear laughter. Not the broken half-hearted chuckle of a killer. Not the condescending bark of a lover who's sick to death of my company. No, laughter like... in a family's home.

I squeeze my eyes shut against a wave of unwanted emotion, and the tears that threaten to follow. What is wrong with me? If I didn't know better, I'd say I didn't want the boys to go.

The next morning, after breakfast, I spend a final few hours on the regulator. I reinforce Ben's too, for good measure.

"Alright," I say. "Your regulators are ready. Time to go. Quick."

"Why quick?" asks Jay, eyes darting, back on alert.

"I'm kicking you out. And myself, too."

"You're kicking yourself out?"

"I'm coming with you," I try to sound confident, like when I used to lead my little brother in the games we played. "You need supplies and a plan if you're going to make it west. I can provide at least part of that. Anyway, this hidden settlement will need books."

I clamp my lips shut against the confession that threatens to follow. That I can't stand to write here alone again, speaking only to killers and characters. That SpaceCorp won't allow a writer to live unmanaged, out in the desert alone. That one of their retrievers knows about me harbouring two fugitives and a bribe only lasts so long.

Ben tilts his head, looking at me with squinted eyes, like he hears my thoughts. He looks at Jay.

"You're right," says Jay. "The new settlement will need books. I hear they're very nourishing."

I exhale.

We spend the day packing supplies and planning our route. Finally, when we're ready, we insert our regulators. Then, we step out into the light of that faraway sun.

"Ok," I say. "Let's go."

We walk under the rocky outcropping and out towards the vast western horizon. I turn and look back at the little cargo container that has been my world ever since I escaped Earth. My refuge, filled with other people's stories. Now it's time to write my own.

See Gaby Brogan's story "The Bookseller of Mars" online at Metaphorosis.
If you liked it, leave a comment. Authors love that!
Remember to subscribe to our e-mail updates so you'll know when new stories are posted.

About the story

"The Bookseller of Mars" was inspired by a daydream about what would happen if someone sensitive, creative, and totally unequipped for the apocalypse managed to get herself onto a survivor spaceship heading to Mars. Where would she be ten years down the road in a lawless new settler society? She'd find herself a peaceful little nook away from the violence, most likely. So, in my mind, this character became a writer and bookseller, catering to the other survivors' need for stories. After a few years of this, I thought this character would be used to dealing with hardened survivors and would become an expert at walking this line between sensitive and guarded. That would be her life. But this just takes us to where the story begins.

When my sister and I were 10 and 11, my parents had two more kids — boys — disrupting our comfortable little all-girls club (+dad). My brothers changed my life with the energy they brought and now, even though we're over a decade apart in age, they're fantastic friends to me as well as great people. Drawing on this, two boys show up at the bookseller's door — changing her comfortable life and giving her a new perspective on family, as well as forcing her out of her shell and towards bold new decisions that shape who she is forever.

A question for the author

Q: What are you reading now?

A: *Other Minds: The Octopus, the Sea, and the Deep Origins of Consciousness.*

If I'm being honest, I've never had enough patience with non-fiction. I would much rather get lost in fantastic new worlds than read more about our own (isn't that what the news is for?!) However, this book was a gift so I was determined to give it a try. And I'm glad I did. The ocean is a fantastic alien world in itself. A few chapters in, I have found a profound new respect for our underwater friends. The idea that intelligent minds, so different from ours, have evolved on our planet is fascinating and tells us more about our own consciousness. Not to mention how inspiring this not-quite-human-intelligence is for a speculative fiction writer! The book is written by Peter Godfrey-Smith, a philosopher of science and scuba diver. As someone who also enjoys scuba diving, his insights have given me a new lens through which to view these explorations.

About the author

Gaby Brogan was raised in the UK and Italy on a steady diet of pasta and science fiction. Usually based in Amsterdam, she's now traveling and working from the road as a freelance copywriter. Whenever she can, she scribbles poetry and fiction, practices yoga, and goes out to explore.

The Antidote for Longing

Karl Dandenell

Part 2

Previously… Lars Bjornsen, the disgraced Swedish imperial poisoner, has been living in exile for the past three years because he failed to assassinate the son of the Russian tsar. One day, a messenger brings a letter from his old friend, the imperial physik Fredrik Magnusson. Fredrik informs Lars that Emperor Gustavus Adolphus is deathly ill and they believe him poisoned, though they cannot be certain. They need Lars' skills to determine a possible antidote before word gets out and triggers a succession crisis since Gustavus has no heir. Lars decides to assist Fredrik and fulfill his duty to the emperor, despite the threat of imprisonment and death that hangs over him every step of the way.

I considered the nondescript servant's entrance of Strömsholm Palace. As much as I wanted to see the brilliant gold-leaf plasterwork of the main doors again, I could appreciate the caution of this approach. With a deep breath, I straightened my cap and pulled the door open, revealing Fredrik Magnusson. He squinted against the daylight. "Lars, is that you?"

"Who else would it be, you old goat?" I said. The imperial physik's white hair and large, droopy mustache were a welcome sight, momentarily pushing aside my worries. His wool coat was dyed a simple green, although his tailor had added intricate patterns of gold thread along each cuff. "For the love of Saint Catherine, Fredrik, let's go inside before my nether regions freeze off."

"You southerners are so delicate," he said.

"Denmark is hardly Iberia."

"*Valkömmen*, my friend!" His strong arms embraced me. "The emperor's condition has not improved," he whispered, his mustache tickling my ear. "I'll tell you more once we have some privacy."

"It's good to see you, too." I held Fredrik a moment longer, then followed him through one of the kitchens, where he handed me a serving basket.

"Get us some *kanelbullar*, would you?" he said in a deliberately casual tone. The nearby tables were covered with trays of marzipan cookies, dried apple tarts, and rolls still warm from the ovens.

"I've never seen so many sweets outside Jultid." My mouth watered. I'd eaten only a spare breakfast and missed lunch due to the messenger's arrival.

"It's been like this for weeks," Fredrik said. "The emperor demands pastries at every meal, and between meals, and sometimes in the middle of the night. No wonder his dyspepsia has returned."

I filled our basket and inhaled deeply. "Oh, I've missed these." Järna's bakers, while skilled, were mere epigones to those of court.

Fredrik appropriated a coffee carafe and porcelain cups, then took me to a small chamber assigned to him. It was warm, with a cheery fire, a writing desk and chair, a bed, and two familiar items: a chaise lounge and a large chest of drawers holding his medical tools and herbs. As a member of court, Fredrik was allotted a large travel allowance of personal baggage. "Not up to the standards of Drottingholm, but comfortable."

"More comfortable than my first fortnight at Järna, I assure you." It had taken me months of wooing patrons before I could afford to replace my furnishings or even adequately heat my house.

He closed the door and poured coffee. "That will put some color in your cheeks."

I hung my coat by the fire. "So, you started a rumor the emperor had dyspepsia and gout?"

"It was Spymaster Viklund's idea," replied Fredrik.

"An excellent idea. Maja's always been clever." Dangerously so. I raised my cup and sipped. "Once the story made the rounds, I suspect the nobles and their respective entourages fled back to Stockholm as soon as they could make their excuses." Gustavus Adolphus's tolerance for fools was low at the best of times. Under duress of illness, he lost all sense of decorum and became the very model of the irrational autocrat his enemies imagined.

"Indeed," said Fredrik. "With only the family servants, guards, and a few senior advisors still in attendance, we may be able to resolve this problem before it becomes a public crisis." He sounded confident but chewed his mustache nervously.

I was once well-acquainted with the emperor's inner circle and maintained a well-annotated mental map of political relationships, much like I had organized my battalions in the Prussian campaigns. Yet it had been three years since my last appearance at court, which meant my intelligence was woefully outdated. As much as I hated to admit it, I had depended extensively on Maja's insight. She'd whispered secrets across the pillow rather than words of love. Now I was left only with Fredrik's gossip. I sighed inwardly. "When did the *actual* illness start?"

"About a week ago. We've been touring the provinces, as one does, taking the measure of the nobles, before the official birthday celebration a week after Epiphany."

I tore a roll in half and dipped it. "I remember Gustavus's sixtieth. Quite the fete." The entire event had been so expensive that every noble was assessed a special levy above and beyond their expected 'gift' to the emperor.

"This one is much worse," said Fredrik, shaking his head. "Days on the road. Nights filled with feasts, concerts, dances, and parties. Even the strongest veteran from the Scottish campaigns would have found the pace challenging, let alone an elderly man who sleeps with eight feather pillows."

I said, "His Majesty used to jest that if the Society of Poisoners could find ways to prolong men's lives as easily as end them, we'd all be rich as Croesus. You poor physiks would have naught to do but pull rotten teeth and treat the pox."

Fredrik frowned at the barb. "As I was saying, His Majesty's personal servants called upon him at the usual hour but could not rouse him. Fearing illness, they summoned me.

"My examination found only a slight fever, though his heart sounded like a newly captured bird flinging itself against its cage. With some reluctance, my suspicions turned to poison."

"As wonderful as it is to see you, my friend, you risked your reputation"—and possibly my life—"by bringing me here. Wouldn't it have been easier to consult… Lord Anders?" I couldn't bring myself to say the *current imperial poisoner.*

Fredrik folded his hands. "Most definitely not. Anders Selberg is dead."

"What?" I set aside my roll, my appetite gone.

"Josef, one of the footman, found him collapsed at his writing desk, a suicide note under his hand."

"Poor *gubbe.*" As much as I'd disliked Anders—he'd always been a status-seeking popinjay—he'd been a member of the Society. At the end of the day, he deserved the benefit of the doubt. I spoke a short prayer to Saint Catherine.

Fredrik said, "My thought is the villain tried to poison the emperor and having failed, took his own life to avoid a lengthy and painful confession at the hands of the spymaster before his eventual execution."

"That's one possibility." Maja might have been a gentle and kind lover, but her public persona lacked mercy. "Another possibility is a larger plot, but Anders wasn't part of it. When he discovered it, the assassins killed him. Or he took his own life out of shame. I probably would." Poisoners swore on their lives to obey and protect their sovereign.

"If that were the case, why didn't he say something?" Fredrik scratched his beard. "*Oj!* There'll be time enough later to invent conspiracies. What we have to do right now is treat the emperor."

"Agreed. I'll need to examine him."

"Ah," said Fredrik. "That might prove difficult. I'm the only one allowed to see him. Spymaster Viklund's orders."

"Where is the emperor now?"

"In the winter guest bedchamber."

"We are in luck, then," I said. "Come with me."

Fredrik set a cocked beaver hat with a gold brooch on his head and followed me down several hallways, passing liveried servants, until we reached a gallery of large tapestries and oil paintings. The entire space was quiet as a church, confirming Birgitta's report that the strolling lute players were idle.

I stopped before a depiction of Vilhelm the Conqueror astride a white warhorse and pointed out the thread's vibrant colors. You could almost see the wind whipping the animal's mane.

The demon lamps cleverly positioned to either side cast almost no shadow, creating an overall effect of afternoon summer light. "The Duke of Uppland spares no expense to display his artwork," I said.

"Or perhaps he brought them in special for His Majesty's visit," said Fredrik. "There's old soot on the wall over here that smells of whale oil."

An older bewigged servant strode through the gallery, his wooden heels clicking against the stone. As he passed, he paused and bowed toward Fredrik. "Good morning, Lord Physik. Do you have a question regarding the tapestry?"

"No, no, I'm fine."

The servant turned to me. "And you, General?"

"None, thank you."

"Very well. If you need anything, please don't hesitate to ask. My name is Oskar." He bowed.

"Wait, I do have a question," I said. "Are you familiar with Madame Torstenson's restaurant near Ulriksdal?"

"I have dined there," said Oskar.

"Tell me," I said, "does she still have a private room for cards?"

"Very much so." He lowered his voice. "Though I am sad to inform you she now requires a fee to play."

"Scandalous!" I dug in my pocket for a silver stag. "Here," I said. "Please partake the next time you're there."

Oskar nodded. "Many thanks, sir." He continued on his way. I waited a good minute, listening carefully to his departing footsteps and my pounding heart.

"Why did you do that?" asked Fredrik. "I thought you wished to remain inconspicuous."

"I gave him a coin and no name. Such transactions are anonymous." There was some risk, admittedly, but it had been so *long* since I'd heard any gossip from Stockholm that I couldn't help myself.

"Let us proceed." I felt the wall along the tapestry's edge until I found a familiar slot. "Here we are." I pressed the recessed keys in sequence. There was a soft click and a panel swung inward, revealing a hidden passageway. "Quickly! I'll be right behind you."

Fredrik ducked under the edge of the tapestry. I slipped in and closed the door behind us. "Bide a moment." On a shelf adjacent to the door, I located a patch box with a goodly supply of char cloth and beeswax candles. A minute later, I'd coaxed enough flame to light a candle.

"Where does this lead?" said Fredrik.

"Several places, including the winter bedchamber," I replied. "When I trained here with Maja, she used to bring secret couriers through or arrange assignations, depending on the visitor."

"You trained with the spymaster herself?" He sounded impressed.

"She wasn't the spymaster then," I said.

"Surely you don't expect me to believe that was the only thing you did together," said Fredrik.

"I will say only we shared common interests," I replied. The Society had taught me the best poisoner is an amalgam of physik and spy, and Maja had been quite willing to explore those territories with me. "Best we keep quiet now."

We soon arrived at a plain wooden door with a dusty brass knob, which I took as a sign that no one had passed this way recently.

Fredrik pressed his ear to the door. "I hear nothing," he whispered, and slowly turned the knob.

We emerged into a room dominated by a large, canopied bed. Upon it lay Gustavus Adolphus, Emperor of Scandinavia and Northern Europe, including Prussia, Austria, and the Netherlands.

Small demon lamps and a banked fire cast a soft glow over the scene. "We're alone," Fredrik said. "Go ahead."

I quickly examined my sovereign. The years since our last meeting had not been kind. His face was thinner and more lined, the skin pale, almost waxy. His pupils were dilated and did not shrink when I brought a lamp close to his face. I also confirmed he was breathing shallowly, though his heart was indeed working harder than it should. *What had they done to him?*

With great care, I tilted the emperor's head and exposed the tongue, which had a peculiar dark coating. Taking my kerchief, I rubbed it over the tongue to get a sample. Finally, I straightened the bedclothes, noting the old man's aroused state.

We returned to the secret passage and I directed Fredrik to another exit that opened into a book-filled chamber: the emperor's traveling library. The glowing coals in the fireplace did little to chase away my chill.

"I fear God will have the emperor all too soon unless I devise an antidote," I said.

Fredrik chewed the edges of his mustache. "You think it's a poison, then."

"It's not one of the Twenty Nine poisons, but it certainly has the *feel* of one," I said. Something about the emperor's condition resonated in memory like a distant church bell, familiar yet quickly fading.

"If you can't recognize the poison, nor I the disease, we are lost," said Fredrik.

"I would give my best winter coat to talk to Lord Anders right now. I'm sure he could enlighten us."

"If you could talk to Lord Anders, the bishop would burn you for a witch," said Fredrik. "However, we might divine something from his room."

An old woman wearing a stained, shapeless dress and worn leather shoes was sweeping up shards of pottery and glass as we entered Anders' chamber. A tall young footman stood nearby, feeding the fire with pages that he tore from a notebook.

"*Javlar!*" shouted Fredrik. *Devils!* "What's going on here, Josef?"

The woman dropped her eyes and bent into a stuttering curtsey, her joints crackling. Josef said, "The chamberlain ordered this chamber cleaned, Lord Physik," and ripped out another page.

"Did he also tell you to destroy imperial records?" I spoke with as much authority as I could muster. "Get out, both of you."

The woman picked up her bucket and broom.

"Leave the bucket," I said. She bobbed her head and departed, followed by the footman, who offered the tattered notebook to me with the barest of bows.

Fredrik closed the door behind them. "I advise we search quickly."

"See what's in the desk," I said. "I'll peruse the wardrobe."

The wardrobe's main compartment held neat stacks of clothing: silk shirts, body linens, and hose. When I dug through the pockets of a sky-blue brocade jacket, I discovered a poisoner's flask, which I pocketed.

On the wardrobe's top shelf, I found Anders' poison kit. Inside lay neat rows of stoppered glass vials. Three vials were missing.

I scanned the remaining labels, deciphering the Society code. "Fredrik, have you found anything?"

He had laid out the desk's contents on the gilt blotter: spare candles, new quills, a small trimming knife with a bone handle, bottles of ink, and a novel. "Nothing interesting, unless you have a fancy for *The Sailor Returns to Tønsberg*." He fanned the pages and found a scrap of parchment serving as a bookmark. "Apparently," said Fredrik, skimming the page, "the titular character is fascinated by the baker's daughter, whose breasts are described in great detail. Ah, the agony of young love." He closed the book. "I'll bet you all the butter in Småland this was written by some poxy clerk whose only experience with women is gazing upon a statue of the Blessed Virgin. Useless. What of the notebook?"

I flipped through the remaining pages. "Mostly the words 'I have failed' and 'forgive me' and some scratched out lines. A draft of his suicide note, one presumes. The fire has the rest.

"Bring over a candle, Fredrik." I borrowed a pair of leather gloves from the wardrobe and carefully shook out the servant's bucket. Fredrik held the flame close, nearly singeing his beard as he leaned in. I picked through the glass until I found the poison kit's missing labels. "Something is amiss."

"How so?"

"This is *Ottoman Madness*, which is quick but agonizing. A poor choice for suicide."

"Perhaps he panicked and made a mistake," said Fredrik.

"Unlikely. A good poisoner always keeps a personal dose of *Dream Caller* or *Cloudless Sky* on hand to avoid capture." *And inevitable questioning.* "And even if Anders didn't, he had *Umber Sorrow* and *Autumn Sunset* in his kit." I shook my head. "As a member of the Society, Anders took an oath to protect the emperor at any cost. He would have given his life to fulfill that oath." I swept the glass into the bucket and stripped off the gloves. "I believe he was silenced to cover the attempted regicide."

"So they may try again," said Fredrik.

"It's what I would do," I admitted. "If His Majesty hadn't banished me, I would have returned to Moscow to finish the mission."

"Lars, please, we must focus." He squeezed my shoulder. "What poison would have manifested such symptoms in the emperor?"

"*Mad Monk* would explain the heartbeat, but the deep sleep is more akin to *Miner's Fate*." An old memory arose, tinged with nostalgia, but I couldn't quite hold it.

"Could we not try treat the emperor for both to be sure?"

"That's not a wise course," I said. "Honestly, I am at loss." My stomach growled.

" 'Hungry is stupid'," said Fredrik, quoting one of our old academy lecturers. "Let's get you a proper meal and then perhaps things will make more sense."

"You're probably right." I picked up the notebook. Fredrik winked and grabbed the novel.

Once we were safely ensconced in Fredrik's chamber, he put the novel on the desk and tossed a log on the fire. I eased onto the chaise and pulled my shoulders back, everything cracking and popping. "Damn that carriage."

"They are difficult on one's bones," said Fredrik. "Do you want a brandy?"

"After some food."

"I'll scavenge something once I check on the empress." He poked the fire. "The fewer people who see you, the better."

"We've been lucky so far," I said. "Why are you seeing the empress? Is she also ill?"

"Tired and irritable. Not sleeping well, apparently," he said. "Until recently, Empress Anna has been visited by her husband most nights on this tour. So says her maid." Fredrik rose and brushed a bit of ash from his trousers. "Throw the bolt behind me. I'll give the academy knock when I get back."

I rapped the chair frame with my knuckles: a six-beat staccato signaling a proctor was patrolling the dormitory.

"Perfect," said Fredrik. "I'll return forthwith."

I bolted the door as instructed, then stretched out, thinking a short rest might restore my wits. When I closed my eyes, though, all I could see was Anders' face stretched in agony after consuming *Ottoman Madness*.

In Lapland, there was a monastery called the Eternal Crevasse. As part of my

Society training, I spent an autumn there studying the monks and their astonishing immunity to seventeen of the Twenty Nine poisons. The key, they said, was an ancient breathing practice and daily recitation of an eight-word Norse prayer handed down by the gods themselves.

For years, the Society had tried to reproduce this secret knowledge. How much easier would assassinations become if the poisoner could drink from the same cup as the target?

The monks taught me the prayer and sat next to me for hours, working my belly like a bellows to infuse me with freezing air and divine presence.

My efforts failed, like the other poisoners before me. Fortunately, my compatriots were able to administer the antidote before the swallow of *Miner's Fate* froze my lungs completely.

Since then, I had occasionally returned to the breathing practice when fatigued or struggling to face another day of false smiles and empty platitudes from my patrons.

I set the candle close by and placed both hands on my belly. With an eye on the flame, I filled and emptied my lungs as forcefully as possible. After two hundred breaths, a great sense of calm descended on me, reminiscent of my first taste of *Dream Caller.*

Dream Caller.

I retrieved Ander's flask from my pocket. When I unscrewed the top, the odor that emerged was not, as I expected, the copper and rosemary of *Dream Caller.* Nor was it the earthy petrichor of *Ottoman Madness.* It was something else entirely: thickly sweet like honey or burned sugar. It was the aroma of Christmas dinner at the Imperial Academy with its giant gingerbread castle and caramel-mortared battlements.

Someone knocked at the door. "Not now!" I rummaged for my kerchief. Held it close to my nose, inhaling deeply. Closed my eyes and slipped into memory.

A party. Music and drunken laughter. Students in their finery, handing out goblets of punch....

The knocking repeated. Six beats.

The memory vanished. "All right!"

I threw open the door. Fredrik stood there, balancing a tray piled with cold meats, breads, cheeses, and more pastries.

"Help me, will you?

I took the tray. He bolted the door, then cleared a space on the desk.

"I bear good tidings!" From his coat, he produced a bottle of brandy and two tiny glasses. "The empress is with child!" he whispered fiercely. He uncorked the brandy, practically dancing.

"Most excellent tidings, sir," I said. "Thank Saint Catherine."

"Indeed. I can't wait to tweak the spymaster's nose. Once the emperor is well, of course." He filled our glasses. *"Skål!"*

"Skål." I drank, then proceeded to layer cheese on bread. "What tweaking would this be?"

He snagged a slice of ham. "She confided her worry that the emperor might be too old to father a child. She hinted— with all the care and subtlety you'd expect from her—that there might be something I could do."

"An aphrodisiac?"

"Clearly." He raised his glass. "I informed her that I was the imperial physik, not some weird woman huddling over a cauldron in the forest. If God wanted the emperor to have another child, He would provide." Fredrik chewed noisily. "The best thing I could do was encourage husband and wife to cleave unto each other. Which they have been."

"Apparently our Lord agreed with your suggestion." I broke open a roll, releasing scents of marzipan and burnt sugar. It smelled like Gustavus's mouth.

"Fredrik?"

"Hmm?" He said, topping up his glass.

"How long has the baker been making extra marzipan rolls? And the other sweetmeats?"

"I'm not sure. Perhaps a few months."

"*After* you had this exchange with Maja?"

"I think so, yes," he said.

The facts were starting to form a worrisome pattern. "When I examined the emperor earlier, did you happen to notice his state of arousal?"

"I took it as a sign of his general health and vitality."

"What about last night, and this morning, before you sent for me? Was he the same?"

Fredrik frowned. "He was, though I fail to see how that matters."

The hairs of the back of my neck rose. "And you're positive the empress is gravid?"

"I wouldn't make a proclamation in Stockholm's central *torget* just yet, but yes, she is. What has the blessed event have to do with the emperor's illness?"

"Because he's been poisoned," I said. *Anders, you fool. What were you thinking?*

He fixed me with a serious look. "But you said it wasn't one of the known poisons."

"I said it wasn't one of the Twenty Nine. Strictly speaking, it's hardly a poison at all. But it is known within the Society." I took a bite of my sandwich. "We call it *Sweet Agony.*"

See parts I and II of Karl Dandenell's story "The Antidote for Longing" online at Metaphorosis.
If you liked it, leave a comment. Authors love that!
Remember to subscribe to our e-mail updates so you'll know when new stories are posted.

Copyright

Title information

Metaphorosis August 2023

ISSN: 2573-136X (online)
ISBN: 978-1-64076-263-3 (e-book)
ISBN: 978-1-64076-264-0 (paperback)

Works of fiction

This book contains works of fiction. Characters, dialogue, places, organizations, incidents, and events portrayed in the works are fictional and are products of the author's imagination or used fictitiously. Any resemblance to actual persons, places, organizations, or events is coincidental.

All rights reserved

Moral rights asserted

Each author whose work is included in this book has asserted their moral rights, including the right to be identified as the author of their respective work(s).

Publisher

Metaphorosis
a magazine of speculative fiction

Metaphorosis Magazine is an imprint of
Metaphorosis Publishing
Neskowin, OR, USA

www.metaphorosis.com

"Metaphorosis" is a registered trademark.

Discounts available

Substantial discounts are available for educational institutions, including writing workshops. Discounts are also available for quantity purchases. For details, contact Metaphorosis at metaphorosis.com/about

Metaphorosis Publishing

Metaphorosis offers beautifully written science fiction and fantasy. Our imprints include:

Metaphorosis Magazine
Plant Based Press
Verdage
Vestige

You can also find us:
Metaphorosis@writing.exchange
@Metaphorosis
www.facebook.com/metaphorosis

Help keep Metaphorosis running by supporting us at
Patreon.com/metaphorosis

See more about some of our books on the following pages.

Metaphorosis Magazine

Metaphorosis
a magazine of speculative fiction

Metaphorosis is an online speculative fiction magazine dedicated to quality writing. We publish an original story every week, along with author bios, interviews, and notes on story origins.

We also publish monthly print and e-book issues, as well as yearly Best of and Complete anthologies.

Come and see us online at magazine.Metaphorosis.com.

Plant Based Press

Vegan-friendly science fiction and fantasy, including anthologies of the year's best SFF stories, from 2016-2020.

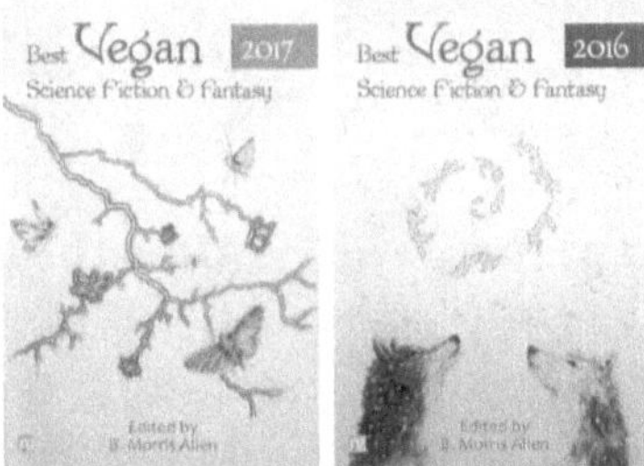

Chambers of the Heart

speculative stories
by
B. Morris Allen

A heart that's a building, a dog that's a program, a woman sinking irretrievably — stories about love, loss, and motion.

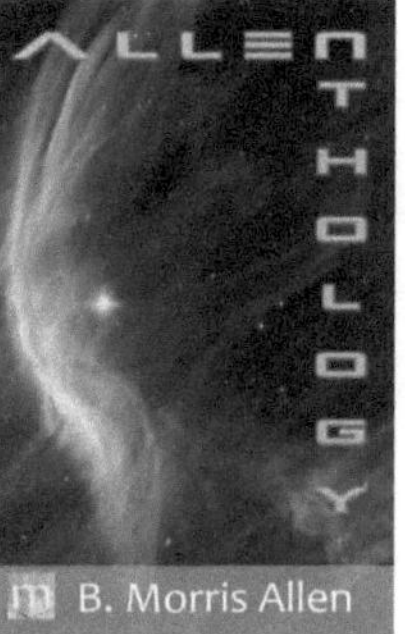

Susurrus

A darkly romantic story of magic, love, and suffering.

Allenthology: Volume I

Including three full collections of SFF stories.

Verdage

Science fiction and fantasy books for writers — full of great stories, often with an additional focus on the craft of speculative fiction writing.

Reading 5X5 x3

Changes

How do stories move from 'maybe' to published?

Here are 15 case studies of stories published in *Metaphorosis* magazine.

Reading 5X5 x2

Duets

How do authors' voices change when they collaborate?

A round-robin of five talented science fiction and fantasy authors collaborating with each other and writing solo.

Including stories by Evan Marcroft, David Gallay, J. Tynan Burke, L'Erin Ogle, and Douglas Anstruther.

Score

an SFF symphony

An anthology with an emotional score from the heights of joy to the depths of despair – but always with a little hope shining through.

Reading 5X5

Five stories, five times

See how different writers take on the same material.

Reading 5X5

Writers' Edition

Two extra stories, the story seed, and authors' notes on writing.

Vestige

Novelettes, novellas, and novels by Metaphorosis authors.

The Nocturnals
Mariah Montoya

**Night is Dangerous.
Day is deadly.**

Where day and night last thirty years, humans move constantly stay ahead of the night and cruel Nocturnals that call it home. But a boy is lost out there.

Joyful Heave

Science fiction and fantasy anthologies with innovative and unusual themes.

Museum Piece
an unusual collection

A gallery of the strange and outrageous

Step right up and enter a world of wonder and oddities! These museums are not your typical tourist traps. From the Museum of Lost Dreams to the Suicide Museum, each exhibit will take you on a journey you won't soon forget.